Dear Taffy and Family

    I'm sorry to have to tell you that my contract with the postal service is up next week and I've decided to retire to Arizona. Until the post office at Windy Bend finds someone to contract for a station here in the valley, You will have to go into town for your mail. It shouldn't be too long — I know they're already taking applications.

    I hope this doesn't incon[venience] you too much. I'v en[joyed] delivering your mail. [']

        All the best —

        Charlie "Red" Wilson

---

show that you have [...]
count three time [...]
e last month. Ti[...]
concerned about [...]
nce recent is [...]
overdrafts la[...]
e look for a [...]
thing to [...]
an do to [...]
learn[...]
a [...]

PS Form 2591, November 1993 (Page 1 of 4)

LINITED STATES POSTAL SERVICE
Application for Contract Station
(Shaded Areas for Postal Service Use Only)
The US Postal Servic[e]
Equal Opportunity Em[ployer]

| Filed For | Filed Application | | Rating | | Date Revie[w] |

To Whom It May Concern:

    Red Wilson has told me about his retiring to the desert and closing this station. I have a large family and we would like to apply for the job of providing that service to our valley. We know the area well and would do a good job of handling the mail.

        Sincerely yours,
        Taffy MacDonald

TAHNEE

NOTHING

TAFFY
(AND HER FAMILY)

OTTO

TORY

BUNNY

MAYBE

WUZZY

PERI

DIGGEDY

TAPS

BUMP

MINKY-WEEZLE

PUSSY

THUMP

JEEP

WILLOW

Special Deliveries

STORY BY ALEXANDRA DAY AND COOPER EDENS

PICTURES BY
ALEXANDRA DAY

HAR   ERS

My heartfelt thanks to the real Taffy, Tahnee, Tory, and their family of animals,
to Garnet and Otto, to Stephen and Kessiah Gordon,
and to Bumble for their cheerful help
—A.D.

For my mother, Garnet, and my father, Otto
—C.E.

Special Deliveries
Text copyright © 2001 by Alexandra Day and Cooper Edens
Illustrations copyright © 2001 by Alexandra Day
Printed in Hong Kong. All rights reserved.
www.harperchildrens.com
Library of Congress Cataloging-in-Publication Data

Day, Alexandra.
Special deliveries / story by Alexandra Day and Cooper Edens ; pictures by Alexandra Day.
p.   cm.
Summary: Taffy and her family deliver the mail for their valley
and write to those who do not receive any mail regularly.
ISBN 0-06-205151-2
ISBN 0-06-205152-0 (lib. bdg.)
[1. Letter carriers—Fiction.]   I. Edens, Cooper.   II. Title.
PZ7.D32915 Sp   2001   00-32035
[E]—dc21

1 2 3 4 5 6 7 8 9 10

First Edition

"Hey, Mom, the post office is on the phone."

"Good news! We've got the job of providing postal service for our valley. We'll have to do some preparation, though, if we're going to do our very best."

"Nope, nothing for her. And Mr. Svenson's house is next, but all he ever gets is 'current occupant' mail."

"Are you sure I can trust you two with this one?"

"Still nothing for Mrs. Trammell, Bunny."

"You know, Mom, some people never get any letters. Don't you think they'd like some?"

"I'm sure they would. Why don't we do something about that? Who doesn't get any mail?"

"There's Mrs. Trammell, old Mr. Svenson, the two new children at the Ramseys', and the student from Nigeria who's living at the Bigelows'."

"It sounds as if there's lots for everybody to do. Let's get busy!"

"Here, Mrs. Trammell, there are several letters for you today."

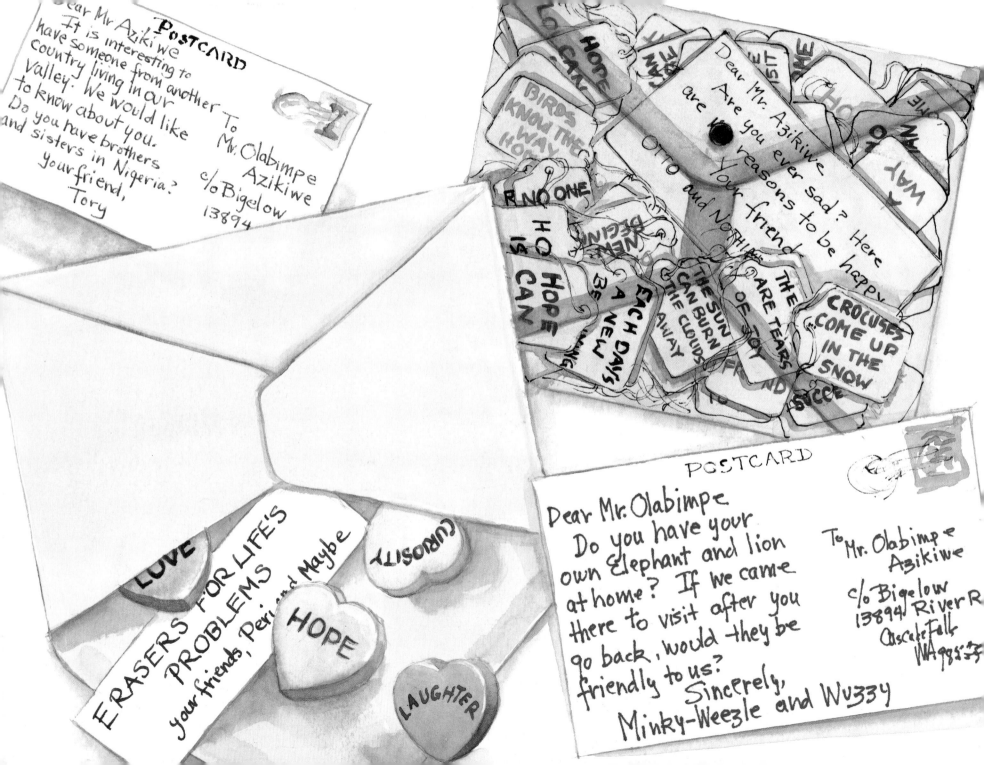

POSTCARD

Dear Mr Azikiwe
It is interesting to have someone from another country living in our valley. We would like to know about you. Do you have brothers and sisters in Nigeria?
your friend,
Tory

To Mr. Olabimpe
Azikiwe
c/o Bigelow
13894

Dear Mr. Azikiwe
Are you ever sad? Here are reasons to be happy Otto and Northal your friends

BIRDS KNOW THE WAY HOME

R NO ONE

HO HOPE IS CAN

HO HOPE IS CAN

THE SUN CAN BURN THE CLOUDS AWAY

EACH DAYS A NEW

BE NEW

THE ARE TEARS OF JOY FRIEND IS

CROCUSES COME UP IN THE SNOW

LOVE

CURIOSITY

HOPE

LAUGHTER

ERASERS FOR LIFE'S PROBLEMS
your friends, Peri and Maybe

POSTCARD

Dear Mr. Olabimpe
Do you have your own Elephant and lion at home? If we came there to visit after you go back, would they be friendly to us?
Sincerely,
Minky-Weezle and Wuzzy

To Mr. Olabimpe
Azikiwe
c/o Bigelow
13894 River R
Cascade Fall
WA 98537

"Another day of good work, everybody.
Come have some cocoa and look at our mail."

"Mom, look at this invitation we got from Mrs. Trammell!"

"We can all go, can't we, Mom?"